The
Magic
Potions
Shop

The
River
Horse

By Abie Longstaff & Lauren Beard:

The Fairytale Hairdresser and Rapunzel

The Fairytale Hairdresser and Cinderella

The Fairytale Hairdresser and Sleeping Beauty

The Fairytale Hairdresser and Snow White

The Fairytale Hairdresser and Father Christmas

The Fairytale Hairdresser and the Little Mermaid

The Fairytale Hairdresser and the Sugar Plum Fairy

The Magic Potions Shop: The Young Apprentice

The Magic Potions Shop: The River Horse

The Magic Potions Shop

The River Horse

Abie Longstaff
&
Lauren Beard

RED FOX

THE MAGIC POTIONS SHOP: THE RIVER HORSE
A RED FOX BOOK 978 1 782 95190 2

First published in Great Britain by Red Fox,
an imprint of Random House Children's Publishers UK
A Penguin Random House Company

Penguin
Random House
UK

This edition published 2015

3 5 7 9 10 8 6 4 2

Penguin Random House is committed to a sustainable future for
our business, our readers and our planet. This book is made from
Forest Stewardship Council® certified paper.

MIX
Paper from
responsible sources
FSC® C018179

Set in Palatino Regular 16/23pt

Red Fox Books are published by Random House Children's Publishers,
61–63 Uxbridge Road, London W5 5SA

www.randomhousechildrens.co.uk
www.totallyrandombooks.co.uk
www.randomhouse.co.uk

Addresses for companies within The Random House Group Limited
can be found at: www.randomhouse.co.uk/offices.htm

THE RANDOM HOUSE GROUP Limited Reg. No. 954009

A CIP catalogue record for this book is available from the British Library.

Printed and bound in Great Britain by Clays Ltd, St Ives plc

For Sam Musgrove
– A.L.

For Dad
– L.B.

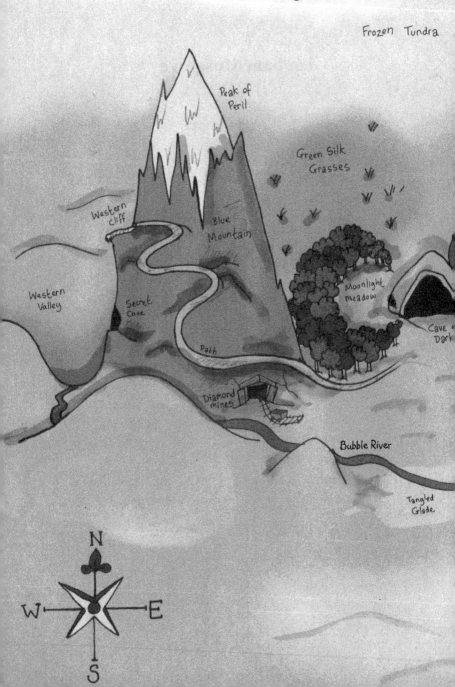

Chapter One

Deep in Steadysong Forest was an enormous tree. It was the biggest tree in the Kingdom of Arthwen and its vast trunk was hollowed out to house a very special shop: the Potions Shop. This shop was where goblins came to get **ExplOding Powder** to help them in the Diamond Mines. It was where dragons bought **Magic Coal** for their belly fire, and where imps came for *Invisible Potion* so they could play all kinds of mischievous tricks.

At the top of the tree were three little bedrooms. In the first one a pixie called Tibben was just waking.

He stretched and yawned. The
sun was already creeping across the
wooden floor and it was time to get
up. Customers would start arriving
soon, travelling from all over
Arthwen to the Potions Shop.

Tibben yawned again. The shop
had been so busy lately! Every day
creatures came, needing creams and
ointments and oils and potions.

Grandpa was the Potions Master.
He was the one
who made all
the different
remedies and
cures. He travelled
the kingdom, from
the Frozen Tundra

to the Parched Desert, visiting creatures and helping them.

Tibben was the Potions Apprentice. It was his job to help Grandpa, to study and to learn. Then, one day, when Grandpa retired, Tibben would take the Master's Challenge to become a Potions Master himself. Tibben was studying hard, practising new potions every day. He had already earned one Glint – the magical sign of potions skill. As he pulled on his cloak, Tibben could see the **Glint** shining out brightly against the plain green fabric. It was only one, but it was a start. Tibben couldn't wait until his cloak sparkled with hundreds of **Glints** of all shapes and sizes, just like Grandpa's. Four more **Glints** to go, Tibben told himself as he opened his door, then I can take the Master's Challenge!

He had promised Grandpa that this morning he would work on *Jumping Potion*, after yesterday's disaster, when he'd added too much **Bouncy Moss**. The potion had only worked on his left shoulder, and he'd spent the whole day twitching like he had fleas.

He tiptoed down the corridor, trying not to wake Grandpa, who had been up till late last night picking **Red-Hot Orchid** in Steadysong Forest. Tibben could hear soft snores coming from behind his door.

In the next room along Tibben could hear Wizz leaping about. He smiled – Wizz could never keep

ZZZZZ...

still! The branches of the tree shook
as she whizzed around, jumping
from bed to sofa to wardrobe to
window. Wizz had only recently
come to live with them, and Tibben
was glad she had settled in so well.
She seemed to love helping in the
Potions Shop, and every day she
was getting better and better at
talking.

He knocked. "Wizz? I'm going down to practise."

"Wizz come! Wizz come!" she cried. She flung open her door. Her huge blue eyes stared up at Tibben and her tail quivered in excitement. "Catch Wizz!" she shouted. She rushed past him and down the spiral stairs in a blur of white fluff.

Tibben laughed and followed her all the way to the shop.

"I'm making *Jumping Potion* again," said Tibben as he lifted his special **Mage Nut** bowl onto the counter. Wizz winked and made her left shoulder twitch. "Very funny," said Tibben. "Hopefully I can get it right this time."

Wizz dashed around the shop fetching all the ingredients for Tibben. She was so quick! She could leap from shelf to shelf in the blink of an eye. Even though there were thousands of jars and bottles and

tubs and pots holding all kinds of plants and seeds and flowers, Wizz could find anything Tibben needed.

"Wow! Thanks, Wizz," said Tibben as she set everything out on the counter. There was the **Bouncy Moss**, a balloon-shaped plant that grew in Moonlight Meadow; and the *Leaping Lily*, which had to

be fished out of Bubble River at dawn while the flower was still sleepy enough to be caught. Wizz had even brought a flagon of **Fire Fuel Hops** down from the very top shelf, holding it in her tail, without spilling a single drop.

Tibben concentrated on mixing the ingredients together.

He was careful not to put in too much **Bouncy Moss** this time, and he chopped up the *Leaping Lily* quickly before it leaped away.

"Hmm," said Tibben, "I wonder how much **Fire Fuel Hops** to add. I might just pop upstairs and ask Grandpa." But Wizz shook her head. "I know, I know . . ."

Tibben wasn't supposed to check everything with Grandpa. He was supposed to try to make the potion himself. He added a few drops of **Fire Fuel Hops**. Then a few more.

Tibben and Wizz peered into the bowl.

"What do you think?" asked Tibben.

"Weeeeez," said Wizz.

"I don't know either," said Tibben. "I'm almost scared to try it."

"Wizz try! Wizz try!"

"Are you sure?"

"Wooz!" Wizz nodded and took a sip.

For a moment nothing happened, but then . . .

Woozoo...

"Woozoo!" cried Wizz as she shot straight up into the air.

"Oops," said Tibben. "Definitely too much **Fire Fuel Hops.**"

"Weeeeeeeee!" Wizz called as she flew round and round the Potions Shop like a balloon running out of air. Tibben could hear the *clink, clink, clink* as she bounced off one jar then another.

14

She was getting
faster and faster
until . . .

Splash!

She landed in a
large tub of Troll
Slime.

Her little head popped out of the
tub, dripping with the bright green
goo. Tibben started to laugh. Wizz
started to laugh.

"Oh, Wizz," gasped Tibben. "What
a mess!" He handed Wizz a towel
to wipe herself down with. Then,
together, they worked to clean up the
shop before customers started
to arrive.

Chapter Two

Ding dong! The bluebell of the Potions Shop rang out.

"Phew!" said Tibben. "Lucky we got everything cleaned in time." He unlocked the heavy front door to greet the first customer of the day.

"Good morning," he said.

On the doorstep crouched a Water Sprite. She was holding her tummy, and her silver wings had turned bright green.

"What's wrong?" asked Tibben.

"Urrrgh . . . my tummy. . ." she groaned.

"Wizz," said Tibben, "please could you fetch some of Grandpa's **Tum Tonic**?" He helped the Sprite into the shop and sat her down on the waiting chair.

"Wooz!" said Wizz. Her eyes scanned the shelves. "Tum wooz!" she cried out happily when she had found what she was looking for. She bounced back down to Tibben.

"Thank you," he said, and opened the little yellow bottle. "This should help," he told the Water Sprite, "it's soft and cooling, and full of **Belly Sage** to make your tummy feel better."

The Water Sprite tipped back her head and drank. Slowly her wings turned from green back to silver.

"Thank you," she sighed. "That's much better. My tummy was so sore."

"Yours is the third tummy we've treated this week, isn't it, Wizz?"

"Third-a-wooz," Wizz agreed.

"I'm beginning to think there's something wrong," said Tibben. He looked at the Water Sprite. She lived underwater in Lake Sapphire, among the *Silver Reeds*. He thought back to the other patients. On Tuesday Wise Nestor, the Bearded Lake-Frog, had come in complaining of

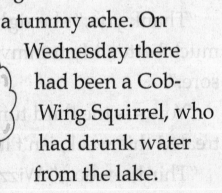

a tummy ache. On Wednesday there had been a Cob-Wing Squirrel, who had drunk water from the lake.

"I need to speak to Grandpa about this right away," said Tibben. As quickly as he could, he climbed the wooden stairs to Grandpa's room.

"Grandpa! Grandpa!" he called as he burst into the room.

"What's wrong, Tibben?" said the Potions Master, propping himself up on his pillow.

Tibben told Grandpa about the Water Sprite. "That's three customers with sore tummies, and they've all been to Lake Sapphire."

"Hmm." Grandpa reached into a secret pocket of his cloak and took out a round object that looked like a pocket watch. He pressed a catch

and it sprang open. This was the *Master's Dial*, which measured Harmony and Blight. The arrow pointed up to H for Harmony when everything was peaceful and calm. But when something was wrong, it moved down towards B for Blight.

Tibben leaned over to look at the arrow. But, oh no! Tibben gasped.

"Grandpa!" cried Tibben. "Blight is growing!"

"Yes," said Grandpa. "I'm afraid it is."

Tibben frowned. "Is it something to do with Lake Sapphire?"

"It might be," said Grandpa. "Why don't you and Wizz go and see?"

"Will you come too?" Tibben asked. "I might not know what to do . . ."

"You'll be fine," said Grandpa, ruffling Tibben's hair.

"But how will I know what's wrong?"

"Look for anything that seems strange or out of place," said Grandpa. "When there's Harmony, everything is as it should be: the rivers, the flowers, the rocks and the animals all look natural and healthy. But when Blight is growing, you'll notice changes. The plants might be wilting, the animals restless, and the air heavy and misty."

"What shall I do to stop the Blight?"

"Just try to help," said Grandpa. "Remember, every time we help someone with our potions, Harmony grows."

"But what if I *can't* help?"

"Tibben. Stop panicking. Close your eyes. Breathe gently in through your nose and out through your mouth. Try to clear your mind."

Tibben did as Grandpa said.

"Better?"

Tibben nodded. "I'll try my best," he said.

"Now, don't forget to pick ingredients on the way," said Grandpa. "We really need more *Mother's Kiss* for **Tum Tonic**, some **Red Clay** for *Sticking Potion*, and we've run out of *Mouse Water* for Shrinking Potion."

Tibben wrote the ingredients down:

Mother's Kiss
Red Clay
Mouse Water

"Ask Wizz to look out for them," said Grandpa. "She's so good at finding things."

"Yes, Grandpa."

"And, Tibben . . ."

"Yes?"

"Keep calm," said Grandpa. "I know you can help."

Chapter Three

Tibben packed his bag carefully. He filled jars with Grandpa's potions and he packed his pockets with handfuls of ingredients – grasses and petals and feathers and vines and seeds and shells and fluff – just in case he had to make his own potions.

"Are you ready, Wizz?" Tibben called, tying his **Mage Nut** bowl onto his bag.

"Ready wooz!" Wizz bounced up.

Tibben and Wizz closed the door of the Potions Shop behind them and set off for Lake Sapphire.

As they walked westward through Steadysong Forest, Wizz darted to and fro, picking Silent Bark for *Invisible Potion*, and *Gumspider Web* for Climbing Potion.

"Save some space in the bag,"
Tibben warned her. "Grandpa has
given me a list of things he needs."
He pulled it out of his bag. "He
wants more ingredients for **Tum
Tonic** . . ." Wizz disappeared into
the undergrowth and popped
up seconds later with pawfuls of
Mother's Kiss.

"Well done!" said Tibben.

"You found it really quickly. I always have to search under the leaves for ages."

"Wooz!" Wizz laughed.

Soon they came to the shore of Lake Sapphire. As they drew closer, Tibben noticed something strange. Usually the area was crowded with birds and hares and fauns and imps and centaurs all queuing to drink the fresh water. But now the shore was empty and silent. Tibben looked at Wizz. Something funny was going on.

Wizz spread her paws open in front of her. "No-weez?"

No-weez?

"Exactly, Wizz," said Tibben. "There's no one here."

When they came to the water, they could tell why. Lake Sapphire was normally sparkly clean, its blue water so clear that Tibben could see all the way to the bottom. Today it was a murky grey, and he couldn't spot any fish or crabs at all.

"I wonder what's going on." Tibben scooped up a jarful of water and held it up to the light . . . The water had a thin film of oil on it. He sniffed – what was that smell?

It was so familiar, but he couldn't quite place it. Wizz took a deep sniff. "Salty wooz," she said. "Water cry."

"You're right, Wizz." Tibben nodded. "The water smells like salty tears."

Tibben opened *The Book of Potions* and thumbed through the pages, looking for the right spell. He came to:

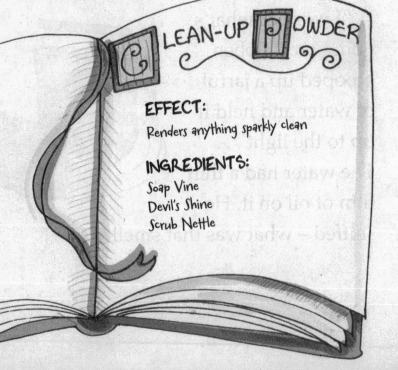

CLEAN-UP POWDER

EFFECT:
Renders anything sparkly clean

INGREDIENTS:
Soap Vine
Devil's Shine
Scrub Nettle

He'd made this potion many times before.

"Wizz," he said, "I've got the Soap Vine and the **Devil's Shine**, but I didn't pack any Scrub Nettle."

"Wizz find!" said Wizz. She jumped up straight away and headed back into the forest.

Tibben got the other ingredients ready. The Soap Vine had to be peeled in thin layers, and the **Devil's Shine** needed podding. Carefully he put them both into his Mage Nut bowl. His tummy jumped in excitement: if he could get this right, if he managed to clean the lake and bring back Harmony, then surely he'd get his next Glint!

"Thanks, Wizz," Tibben said, as she bounced back with the **Scrub Nettle**. He tore it up carefully and added it to the mixture. He stirred everything round three times and watched the ingredients form a light powder. It looked good! He put the powder in a jar and took just what he needed for the lake.

"Here we go," said Tibben, scattering the powder over Lake Sapphire.

Instantly the water turned from dull grey to bright, clear blue. "Yes!" he shouted, excitedly.

"Woozoo!" cheered Wizz.

Tibben looked down for his second Glint. Where was it? He twisted and turned to try to see it on his cloak.

"Huh?" he said. "I didn't
get one."

"Water weez!" cried Wizz
suddenly, and Tibben looked back
at the lake. It had turned grey again!
All the sparkle had gone and it was
cloudy once more.

"What in the kingdom is going
on?" said Tibben.

Chapter Four

Tibben and Wizz walked slowly around Lake Sapphire, trying to see what could be turning the water grey. They looked for something floating in the water, or signs of damage at the shore, but there was nothing to be seen.

Soon they came to Bubble River, the great rushing river that flowed all the way from Blue Mountain, through the Tangled Glade, into

Lake Sapphire, under the Troll Hills, and out to the Fickle Ocean. But today it looked very different. Today the mighty river was moving really slowly, and it was gloopy and grey.

Wizz sniffed. "Salty wooz," she said. "Same same."

Tibben nodded. Wizz was right – the river water smelled just like the lake water.

"Hmm," he said. "Something's coming down the river and making the lake water dirty. And if the river isn't flowing through the lake properly, the dirt won't wash away. We have to follow Bubble River to find out what's going on."

He pulled out the map. "I don't know where the problem is, but let's start by walking to the Tangled Glade. I've always wanted to go there!"

Wizz jumped up and down in excitement. Tibben grinned at her. They'd heard Grandpa talk about the Tangled Glade. It was a magical

place, hidden by Vine Curtain
and full of special creatures and
plants. Grandpa had told Tibben
all about the enormous Horned
Butterflies and the Whistle Birds,
the green Fizzy Ferns and the bright
Patchwork Flowers. Tibben couldn't
wait to go!

They followed the river uphill,
walking along the bank and
watching for changes in the water.
Every now and then Wizz would
sniff the air, shriek, and jump into
a bush or feel under a log to collect
all kinds of seeds and leaves that
Tibben had never seen before. His
bag was getting full!

All of a sudden, Wizz sniffed and leaped into a hollow log. Tibben heard a squeak and then a louder squeak, and he realized that Wizz was stuck! Her tail was high in the air and her white fluffy bottom was wriggling about as she tried to get free. Tibben laughed and yanked her out of the tree. They fell back into a heap.

"Wooz!" said Wizz, shaking her fur. She proudly showed Tibben the yellow **Honey Berries** she had found.

"Yum," said Tibben. "I love **Honey Berries!**"

Wizz shoved a pawful into her mouth and munched on them happily.

On they went. Tibben sang songs as they walked and Wizz squeaked in the choruses.

Soon they came to a little pond. Tibben checked the map.

"Mouse Pond!" he cried. "We're near Vine Curtain now!"

Tibben sat down on the riverbank for a little rest. The river water was still cloudy and stagnant. As he stared into the river, he noticed a school of Silver Fish struggling to swim through the gloop.

"Poor you," he said, and the Silver Fish looked up.

"Here . . ." said Tibben. "I've got something that could help." He reached into his bag for Grandpa's *Swim Fast Gel* and poured the cool gel into the water over the fish. They shot back and forth at top speed and waved their tails in gratitude. The biggest fish swam over and gave Tibben three of his Silver Scales.

"Thank you!" said Tibben. The scales might be useful for something later. He showed Wizz and her eyes lit up.

"Good wooz!" she said. She bent down and scooped up a jarful of **Quick Sand** from the bottom of Mouse Pond so they could make some more *Swim Fast Gel* if they needed it, and took some *Mouse Water* for Grandpa's Shrinking Potion.

"Great," said Tibben, packing it into his overflowing bag. "We've nearly got everything

Grandpa wanted now. Just the **Red Clay** to go, I think. Now come on! I can't wait to get past Vine Curtain!"

They ran round the pond as fast as they could. Soon they came to a wall of vines that ran right across the river. Hundreds of green strands hung down, hiding the world behind. It looked like a dead end.

"Vine Curtain!" cried Tibben. "Wooz!"

Carefully, Tibben parted the greenery – and suddenly he could see further downriver, into the Tangled Glade. His heart was pounding. He took a deep breath and stepped through the vine.

Chapter Five

Tibben looked around. The Tangled Glade looked nothing like Grandpa's stories. The Fizzy Ferns were brown at the edges. The Patchwork Flowers hung limply from their vines. There was no sign of the famous Horned Butterflies, and no sound of Whistle Birds.

Something was wrong.

"Weez!" Wizz pointed to some Glade Mussels. They were waving their shells in the shallows. Tibben looked closely – their pearls were a funny colour. Normally Glade Mussels had beautiful shiny-bright pearls, but the dirty river water had made these dull and drab.

Tibben reached into his bag and pulled out Grandpa's **Glitter Dust**, sprinkling it over the pearls so they shone like tiny moons. The Glade Mussels clapped their shells in thanks and gave him one of their **Glade Pearls**.

"Thank you," he said.

As they walked into the glade,

the air grew thicker and heavier. With every step Tibben felt like he was dragging his foot through porridge.

Tibben and Wizz were quieter now, speaking only when they needed to. There was no singing, and it felt like all the fun of the journey had gone.

"Watch where you're going, Wizz," said Tibben as she nearly tripped him up for a second time. Wizz didn't hear him. She was too busy reaching under a log.

"Stop it, Wizz," said Tibben crossly. "We're supposed to be getting **Red Clay** – "that's what Grandpa needs. We haven't got space for all these extra leaves you're finding. No, I don't want more silly **Honey Berries**," he added as Wizz offered him a pawful.

She shrugged. Then, to Tibben's annoyance, she suddenly stopped walking – and he bumped straight into the back of her.

"Wizz!" he complained. But Wizz wasn't listening. Her nose was turned up and she was sniffing the air. Her whiskers went taut and her fur stood up.

"What is it?" said Tibben, but Wizz didn't answer. She darted across to a rock at the river's edge and turned it over. Underneath was an odd-looking plant. It was bright

green and made of long feathery strands like floppy spaghetti. Wizz began to pull them up.

"No," said Tibben. "No way, Wizz. We've got too many plants to carry already. That one isn't even on Grandpa's list."

Wizz looked at him. "Wizz carry!" she said. "Pleas-weeze."

"Oh, all right," said Tibben grumpily.

Wizz wound the green spaghetti strands round and round to make herself a hat.

Tibben sighed. Wizz was so silly sometimes. They had a job to do.

Who knew how long it would take them to clear up the lake, and here was Wizz messing around eating berries, making hats and picking plants they didn't even need.

Chapter Six

On went Tibben and Wizz, trudging
deeper and deeper into the Tangled
Glade. The air was so heavy and
still! Tibben wiped his sweaty brow.

"Let's stop for a minute," he
gasped, sitting down on a giant
mushroom. Even Wizz was tired.
She had stopped leaping about and
her tail was hanging low in the
undergrowth.

Tibben put his head in his hands.

He had started to worry. They had walked so far! What if he couldn't fix the problem? He shivered. He felt sad inside – sad and empty and cross.

Wizz lifted her paw through the thick air and picked another pile of **Honey Berries**.

"Wizz!" shouted Tibben. "I told you to stop picking berries!"

According to the map, they were now in the heart of the Tangled Glade.

An enormous blue Horned Butterfly flapped slowly by, twisting in and out of the long vines. It came to the river to drink, but the water was so cloudy and gloopy it gave up and flew away sadly. Tibben dropped his head. He still hadn't found the reason for the polluted river.

Just then, he heard a low sob. His ears pricked up. "What was that?"

"Weez?" Wizz had heard it too.

They followed a bend in the river and there, sitting in the water, was a large creature. It had creamy skin and a long neck. Tibben gasped.

It was the River Horse!

Grandpa had showed him drawings of this unique creature, but Tibben had never thought he would actually get to meet him.

Grandpa had told him that the River Horse was wild and strong, and could be found galloping through the rivers, using his magic to make the waters flow throughout the kingdom. In each of his hoofs was a special *Moon Pearl*. These gave the River Horse his strength and power and they helped to churn up the water, refreshing it and making it sparkle with life.

"The River Horse has a special role in keeping Harmony in the waters of the kingdom," Grandpa had said. "He is a magical creature, and you must treat him with respect."

The drawings in Grandpa's book

had shown the
River Horse standing tall
and proud, glowing with a silver
light. But the River Horse looked
nothing like he did in the drawing.
He seemed weak and tired. His
silver mane hung dully against his
coat. He was lying low in the water,
too feeble to gallop anywhere.

Slowly the River Horse lifted his head to look at Tibben. His huge black eyes were heavy with sadness, and tears ran down his face and spilled into the water; big salty drops that flowed down Bubble River all the way to Lake Sapphire.

"Oh!" cried Tibben. He turned to Wizz. "Wizz," he whispered, "I think the tears of the River Horse are making the water dirty."

Wizz nodded. "Horse sad," she said.

Tibben moved towards the River Horse carefully so as not to frighten him. Remembering what Grandpa had said, he bowed low.

"Hello," he said softly, "I am Tibben. I come from the Potions Shop. I'm not the Potions Master, but I can try and help." He showed the River Horse the **Glint** on his cloak. "What's wrong?"

The River Horse looked at Tibben through his tears. Then he flipped over in the water. For a moment

Tibben thought he was going to swim away, but instead the great horse lifted his hooves in the air to show Tibben. In three of the hooves Tibben saw the soft light of a *Moon Pearl* glowing blue, green and silver. But the fourth hoof was empty – the *Moon Pearl* was gone!

Tibben gasped. Without the four *Moon Pearls* the River Horse would have no power to keep the waters moving and refreshing. No wonder the river wasn't flowing! No wonder the tears hadn't washed away!

The River Horse started to cry again.

"We've got to find your *Moon Pearl*," Tibben said. He scanned the water. "Could it be in the river?"

But the River Horse shook his head sadly.

"In the glade?"

But again the horse shook his head.

"If you've looked everywhere, there must be something else I can do," said Tibben. He picked up *The Book of Potions* and looked under M.

Monster Fur Cream
Mop Dance Gel

There was **Monster Fur Cream** and Mop Dance Gel but no Moon Pearl.

"There's nothing here," said Tibben. He sat down hard on the ground. What should he do now?

Chapter Seven

Tibben sighed.

Nothing was right. Everything felt wrong and out of place. The River Horse was so sad about losing his Moon Pearl. Tibben had to get it back – but how? Oh, why hadn't Grandpa come? Tibben put his head in his hands. Now he was all alone and he had no idea what to do.

Just then he felt a little paw on his shoulder. He looked up – Wizz!

Of course! Wizz was there too.

"Oh, Wizz," he said, "I'm sorry I was grumpy with you! I'm so glad you're here." He gave Wizz a hug and, as he touched her soft fur, he remembered what Grandpa told him to do whenever he felt panicky:

Close your eyes, breathe gently in through your nose and out through your mouth. Try to clear your mind.

Tibben breathed in and out until he felt calmer. He snuggled into Wizz's fur and slowly he began to feel better.

"I'm going to look in here again," he said, holding up *The Book of Potions*. He turned the pages one by one until, under E, he found:

ELIXIR OF MOON PEARL

EFFECT:
Creates one Moon Pearl

INGREDIENTS:
Silver Scales, Glade Pearl
Honey Berries, Secret Kelp

Tibben already had the **Silver Scales** from the Silver Fish he had helped, and the **Glade Pearl** from the Glade Mussels. Wizz handed him the **Honey Berries,** and Tibben blushed as he remembered how mean he had been to her for picking them.

"Kelp weez?" said Wizz, pointing to *The Book of Potions*.

"I don't know what *Secret Kelp* is either," said Tibben. He turned to the back of the book to look in the glossary:

Secret Kelp

Rare ingredient for highly specialized potions. Grows in hidden location.

Tibben sat back on his heels. "How are we going to find it?" he said.

Wizz was already darting about, jumping up tree trunks and disappearing down holes. Tibben joined her, reaching as high as he could into bushes and searching with his hand in the gloopy water. It was difficult – for once there was no drawing in *The Book of Potions* showing what the plant looked like. But Wizz seemed to know which plant it *wasn't*. She kept sniffing and touching leaves, then shaking her head.

"No weez."

Tibben hoped Wizz knew what she was doing, because he really had no idea.

Chapter Eight

Tibben looked over at the River Horse. The great creature had laid his creamy head on the bank of the river to watch the hunt for *Secret Kelp*. His eyes were tired and red from crying. Tibben crossed his fingers, hoping that Wizz could find the one last ingredient to make the missing pearl.

Wizz was still leaping about, searching under rocks and moss.

Her fur kept falling into her eyes, so she lifted her paw to tuck it under the hat she had made out of plant strands. The second her paw touched the hat, her whiskers went taut and her fur stood up. She gave a loud "Wooz!"

"What is it?" Tibben looked up from the bushes. Wizz was dancing around in excitement, pulling her hat apart.

"Wizz kelp! Wizz kelp!" she was shrieking, holding out bits of her hat.

"Is that it?" Tibben was doubtful. "The green spaghetti stuff you used to make your hat? Are you sure that's *Secret Kelp*, Wizz?"

"Yes wooz," she nodded firmly.

Tibben didn't know what to do. "The thing is," he told Wizz, "we only have one **Glade Pearl**. If we get the potion wrong, we can't try again."

Wizz looked him steadily in the eye. "Kelp wooz," she said.

Tibben took a deep breath. He looked at his friend. He knew how good Wizz was at finding plants: she had found that *Mother's Kiss* straight away, and the Quick Sand. She had been right to pick the **Honey Berries**, and had insisted on keeping the funny spaghetti plant she was now holding in her paw. He had to trust her.

"OK, Wizz." he said, "Let's make this potion!"

One by one, Tibben put all the ingredients into his **Mage Nut** bowl. He mashed down a **Silver Scale** with his spoon, and broke up the

Honey Berries. He added the strands of *Secret Kelp* bit by bit. What was the mixture supposed to look like? There were no instructions, and Grandpa wasn't here to tell him what to do. He looked into the bowl. He looked over at the River Horse; at his silver mane and his creamy skin.

"Hmm . . . more Silver Scale," he muttered to himself, and added another handful, and another, until . . .

"There," said Tibben, "I think

that's right." He looked at Wizz,
then at the River Horse. He picked
up the shiny white **Glade Pearl** . . .

"Here we go," he said, and
dropped it in.

Chapter Nine

Tibben and Wizz peered into the **Mage Nut** bowl. Tibben swished the **Glade Pearl** around in the mixture. Then he put in his hand and lifted the pearl out. He couldn't wait to see it! He held his breath while the mixture dripped away. Had the Elixir worked?

The pearl glowed blue and green and silver.

He had done it! He had made
a Moon Pearl!

"Yes!" cheered Tibben.

"Woozoo!" Wizz shouted.

The River Horse held out his
empty hoof and the Moon Pearl
fitted in perfectly. The horse
lifted his head. Already he
looked stronger. His eyes lit up
in happiness and his silver mane
shone brightly.

The River Horse stood up in
the water. Tibben gasped.
Upright, the horse towered
over him, shining creamy
and silver. He tossed his
head proudly and stamped
his hooves in the river. Then

he reared up on his hind legs,
and there was a giant splash as he
thundered down. Tibben felt the
spatter of river spray. He felt so
tiny against the power of the River
Horse. Grandpa was right – the
horse was truly magical!

As the horse stamped, the river began to churn and flow. Already it was starting to refresh itself, but there was one thing Tibben could do to help. He opened the jar of Clean-up Powder and poured the last handful into the water.

The River Horse lifted his hooves one by one and stamped down hard. The water began to foam, and then cleared as it grew cleaner. The River Horse galloped faster and faster, and the Clean-up Powder was pushed down the river, through the Tangled Glade, heading past Vine Curtain and on towards the lake.

"That's wonderful!" said Tibben. Already he felt happier and lighter. The air seemed to clear, and all of a sudden, hundreds of Whistle Birds flew down to the water, singing and chirping as they drank the cool clean water. Tibben smiled to see them so excited.

The River Horse lowered his body and motioned with his head for Tibben and Wizz to climb on his back. They looked at each other. Did he really mean to give them a ride?

"Really?" asked Tibben, and the great horse nodded.

Tibben bowed again and gently climbed onto the horse until he was sitting right up high. The silvery hide felt cool and soothing against his legs. Tibben gripped the shimmering mane tightly and tucked Wizz in the crook of his elbow. She wrapped her tail around his wrist to help her hold on.

The River Horse gave a whinny in warning, and then— *whoosh!* They were off!

Through the river they rushed. As the River Horse stamped, the water churned under his hooves and the Clean-up Powder flowed on and on. The River Horse began to gallop faster and faster. He leaped and spun about as he ran, and Tibben had to hold on tight. They flew at top speed through the glade.

Vines and branches flicked by in flashes of green and yellow.

They came to Vine Curtain and whipped through the strands, bursting out into Mouse Pond.

"Wheeeeee!" cried Tibben.

"Woooooz!" shouted Wizz.

Finally . . . **Splash!**

They landed in the bright blue waters of Lake Sapphire.

"That was amazing!" cried Tibben. "Thank you!" He couldn't wait to tell Grandpa that Wizz had found *Secret Kelp*, he had made a *Moon Pearl*, and that now they had taken a ride on the River Horse! He looked at the beautiful lake. It sparkled in the light, and he could see all the way to the bottom, to the *Silver Reeds* where the Water Sprites lived.

Tibben and Wizz danced on the riverbank.

"We did it!" Tibben cried. "We all did it together!"

"Woozoo!"

The River Horse watched them,
his eyes shining brightly. Then
he lifted his enormous head and
gave a loud *"Neigh!"* which
startled Tibben. Something
was happening . . .

After a moment, the air was filled with a flapping, stamping, scratching, splashing noise. The creatures had come back! They had heard the call of the mighty River Horse, and now they were rushing to the

lake to drink. They lifted
their heads, calling and
hooting and barking
and chirping their
thanks to Tibben and the
River Horse.

Tibben looked around
the lake – everyone was
happy and everything felt right.
Harmony was back! His heart filled

with pride. He turned and
looked into the River Horse's
huge black eyes. The horse
nodded at Tibben, and then he
was gone – swimming away up
Bubble River and over all the
streams and tributaries in the
kingdom to make sure they
were flowing well.

Tibben waved till the horse
was out of sight. "Wow," he
breathed. "We actually met the
River Horse!"

"Horse wooz." Wizz nodded.
Then, "Weez!" She pointed at
something on Tibben's cloak.

He pulled the cloak round –
and found a Glint! He'd earned

his second one! This **Glint** looked different to the first. It was *Opal* level – dark blue and shaped like an egg. Tibben stared deep into its centre.

He touched the edge of the **Glint** to hear the soft hum it made when he rubbed it, and twisted his cloak this way and that to watch it sparkling in the light.

Wizz clapped her paws.

"I know!" said Tibben. "My second Glint!" He grabbed her paw. "Come on," he said. "Let's go home. I have so much to tell Grandpa."

Chapter Ten

At the Potions Shop, Grandpa was waiting for them.

"Well done!" he said, and opened his arms wide.

"What does the *Dial* say?" asked Tibben. He couldn't wait to know.

"Harmony!" the Potions Master exclaimed, grinning, and Tibben smiled back.

"Look, Grandpa . . ." Tibben proudly showed him the shiny new *Glint*.

"Only three more to go," laughed the old pixie. "Now come on, I want to hear everything." He lifted Tibben onto the wooden counter and sat himself down in the waiting chair. Wizz balanced on a tall blue bottle containing *Mouse Water*, for making *Shrinking Potion*.

"Well . . ." Tibben began.

He told Grandpa all about the lake, about following Bubble River, about Vine Curtain and the Tangled Glade and about the River Horse.

"Goodness," said Grandpa, "it's been many years since I last saw the River Horse! He doesn't show himself often, Tibben." He smiled. "He must have sensed something special in you."

Tibben blushed. He told Grandpa about the missing *Moon Pearl* and showed him the page in *The Book of Potions*.

"This is what I had to make, Grandpa. See – we had to find *Secret Kelp* and it wasn't listed anywhere."

"*Secret Kelp?*" said Grandpa. "That's a very rare ingredient indeed. Yes. That's very special."

"Wizz kelp! Wizz kelp!" Wizz cried in excitement. She couldn't keep still any more and was leaping about from bottle to jar to urn.

"Wizz found it," said Tibben. "She knew it was *Secret Kelp.*"

"Did she now?" said Grandpa, looking at Wizz closely.

"I didn't believe her at first," Tibben admitted, "but she was right."

"Come here, little Wizz," said Grandpa. "I've been watching you for some time. I've seen how easily you can find ingredients in the

Potions Shop. I've seen how quickly you can dive into the water or reach into the undergrowth to find exactly what we need. Yes.

I've been wondering something for a while, and now that you have found *Secret Kelp*, I think I've worked something out."

Tibben and Wizz looked at each other. What was Grandpa going to say?

"Wizz," Grandpa said, looking into her huge blue eyes, "I think you are a Gatherer."

"Gath-a-weez?" asked Wizz.

"Huh?" said Tibben. "What's a Gatherer?"

Grandpa sat back in his chair. "Gathering is a very rare gift." he said. "It means that Wizz can find plants and berries and seeds that no other creature can."

"Wow!" breathed Tibben, looking at Wizz. For once she was standing stock still, her tail pointing up in the air as she listened to Grandpa.

"There hasn't been a Gatherer for a long time," Grandpa continued.

"Not for hundreds of years. Wizz is something very special."

Tibben was bursting with pride. He knew in his heart that Grandpa must be right – Wizz could find anything! She *must* be a Gatherer!

"Now, Wizz," Grandpa explained, "you can't be an Apprentice because there is no Gathering Master around to teach you." Wizz nodded sadly. "But I will help you," Grandpa went on, and Wizz perked up.

"I'll help too," said Tibben.

"Wooz!" said Wizz.

"Together we will make sure you practise your gift," said Grandpa. "It's far too precious to waste.

A Gatherer! In my lifetime! How wonderful!"

Tibben hugged his fluffy friend.

"I always knew you were special, Wizz," he said.

Wizz squeaked happily and curled her tail around his neck.

"Right," said Grandpa.

"Back to work. Customers could come in at any moment needing help. Tibben, you need to practise making that *Jumping Potion*. Wizz, could you find me the jar of **Bouncy Moss**?"

"Wooz!" squeaked Wizz. She knew exactly where it was.

Potions

Extracts from *The Book of Potions:*

Clean-up Powder
Effect: Makes anything sparkly clean
Ingredients:
- Soap Vine
- Devil's Shine
- Scrub Nettle

Climbing Potion
Effect: Increases climbing skill for two hours
Ingredients:
- Gumspider Web
- Troll Slime

Elixir of Moon Pearl
Effect: Creates one Moon Pearl
Ingredients:
- Silver Scales
- Glade Pearl
- Honey Berries
- Secret Kelp

Exploding Powder
Effect: Causes any substance to explode
Ingredients:
- Jumping Flint
- Fire Seeds
- Red-Hot Orchid

Glitter Dust
Effect: Rubbing with this dust increases sparkle and shine
Ingredients:
- Diamond Powder
- Dew Drops
- Rainbow Blossom

Invisible Potion
Effect: Makes anything invisible for three hours
Ingredients:
- Chameleon Claw
- Glass Pearl
- Silent Bark

Jumping Potion
Effect: Makes drinker jump for 12 hours
Ingredients:
- Bouncy Moss
- Leaping Lily
- Fire Fuel Hops

Magic Coal
Effect: Stimulates fire breath
Ingredients:
- Goblin Coal
- Red-Hot Orchid

Monster Fur Cream
Effect: Makes fur extra thick and hairy
Ingredients:
- Yowl Seed
- Fluff Stalk

Mop Dance Gel
Effect: Makes the drinker dance and shake their hair
Ingredients:
- Mop Willow
- Jumping Flint

Shrinking Potion
Effect: Makes the drinker shrink in size for 10 minutes
Ingredients:
- Vary Violet
- Mouse Water
- Low Root

Sticking Potion

Effect: Sticks anything to anything
Ingredients:

- Gumspider Web
- Red Clay
- Troll Slime

Swim Fast Gel

Effect: Increases swimming speed by 1000 times for one hour
Ingredients:

- Quick Sand
- Flipper Weed

Tum Tonic

Effect: Comforts any sore tummy
Ingredients:

- Belly Sage
- Mother's Kiss

Ingredients

Extracts from
The Glossary of Magic Ingredients

Belly Sage
Grows on Cape of Waves on Eastern Shores. Minty flavour.
Used for **Tum Tonic**

Bouncy Moss
Grows in Moonlight Meadow and Steadysong Forest. Look for
green curled springs. Used for **Jumping Potion**

Chameleon Claw
Granted by Rainbow Chameleons on Blue Mountain after a
favour is performed. Used for **Invisible Potion, Disappearing
Potion** and **Camouflage Potion**

Devil's Shine
Bright shining plant – requires podding. Grows in Western
Valley. Used for **Clean-up Powder**

Dew Drops
Collect from Moonlight Meadow. Used for **Glitter Dust** and
Shine Potion

Diamond Powder
Made from grinding diamonds from the Diamond Mines. Used
for **Glitter Dust, Sharpening Ointment** and **Shine Potion**

Fire Fuel Hops
Given by Sand Elves in the Parched Desert. Used for **Jumping
Potion**

Fire Seeds

Pick these from the Burning Flower in the Parched Desert. Used for **Fire Dance Potion, Super Strength Potion** and **Exploding Powder**

Flipper Weed

Wide yellow plant. Grows in Lake Sapphire. Used for **Swimming Potions**

Fluff Stalk

Grows in the Frozen Tundra. White furry plant. Used for **Monster Fur Cream**

Glade Pearls

Given by Glade Mussels in the Tangled Glade in exchange for **Glitter Dust**. Used for **Elixir of Moon Pearl**

Glass Pearl

Fish for these in Lake Sapphire. Found in transparent oysters. Key ingredient in **Invisible Potion, Disappearing Potion** and **Camouflage Potion**

Goblin Coal

Given by Thunder Goblins under Blue Mountain in exchange for **Exploding Powder**. Key ingredient in making **Magic Coal**

Gumspider Web

Found in Steadysong Forest. Take one strand at a time only. Used for **Sticking Potion, Climbing Potion** and **Tidy Thread**

Honey Berries

Edible berries. Grow in the Tangled Glade. Used to make **Elixir of Moon Pearl**

Jumping Flint

Found in the Diamond Mines under Blue Mountain. Silver stone. Used in **Fire Dance Potion, Mop Dance Gel** and **Exploding Powder**. Beware – this stone will leap about once cut

Leaping Lily

Grows in Bubble River. Spotty purple flower. Used for **Jumping Potion**

Low Root

Found in Moonlight Meadow. Used for **Shrinking Potion**

Mop Willow

Grows in the Tangled Glade. Long thin plant. Used for **Mop Dance Gel**

Mother's Kiss

Grows in Steadysong Forest. Soft warm pink flower. Used for **Pain Relief Potions**

Mouse Water

Collect from Mouse Pond. Used for **Shrinking Potion**

Quick Sand

Covers the ground at Mouse Pond. Beware. Used in all **Speed Potions** and **Ten Legs Potion**

Rainbow Blossom

Grows in Moonlight Meadow. Plant of seven colours. Used for **Glitter Dust** and **Shine Potion** and for **Beauty Potions**

Red Clay

Found at the bottom of Lake Sapphire and Bubble River. Used for **Sticking Potion**

Red-Hot Orchid

Grows in Steadysong Forest. Ruby coloured petals. Do not touch the leaves. Used in **Fire Dance Potion**, **Exploding Powder** and for making **Magic Coal**

Scrub Nettle

Grows in Steadysong Forest. Beware of its sting. Used for **Clean-up Powder**

Secret Kelp

Rare ingredient for highly specialized potions. Grows in a hidden location

Silent Bark

Peeled in Steadysong Forest from the hollow Silent Bark Tree. Key ingredient in **Invisible Potion**, **Disappearing Potion** and **Camouflage Potion**

Silver Reeds

Grow underwater in Lake Sapphire. Used for **Mirror Gel**

Silver Scales

Given by Silver Fish in The Tangled Glade in exchange for **Swim Fast Gel**. Used to make **Elixir of Moon Pearl**

Soap Vine

Grows on Troll Hills – look for distinctive foaming green plant.
Used for **Clean-up Powder**

Troll Slime

Grows under bridges in Troll Hills. Used for **Sticking Potion**,
Climbing Potion and **Tidy Thread**

Vary Violet

Found in Frozen Tundra. Used for **Change Potions**

Yowl Seed

Furry Yowl Plant grows in the Green Silk Grasses. Distinctive
orange and black stripy fur. Used for **Language Potions** and
Monster Fur Cream

Tibben's adventure continues
– read on for a sneak peek of

The Magic Potions Shop

The Ice Star

Chapter One

The Kingdom of Arthwen was
huge. It spread from the Frozen
Tundra in the north to the
Parched Desert in the south; from
the Fickle Ocean in the east all the
way to Western Valley.

In the middle of the kingdom,
just by Lake Sapphire, was
Steadysong Forest; the home
of a very special tree. This tree
was the largest in the kingdom.

At the top was a little house with three bedrooms: one for Grandpa, one for Wizz and one for Tibben. At the base, hollowed out inside the trunk, was a very unusual shop. The shop sold potions. Creatures came here from miles around to get *Super Strength Potion* or **Arm Stretch Cream** or even **Never-ending Chocolate Powder**!

Grandpa was the Potions Master and he could mix any potion. He wore a cloak covered in hundreds of Glints, the magical sign of potions skill. The Glints were all different shapes and sizes and they sparkled in the light whenever Grandpa moved.

Tibben was the Potions Apprentice.
He was learning how to make
potions to help all the different
creatures, and keep Harmony in the
Kingdom. So far he had earned two
shiny Glints for his cloak. One Glint
was shaped like a hexagon and the
other one looked like a dark blue
egg. Tibben was so proud of them!
He only had three more Glints to
go before he could take the Master's
Challenge to become a Potions
Master just like Grandpa. He was
training every day. Not all his potions
worked yet. His Cat Language Potion
made him moo all day and his Long
Beard Gel seemed to only affect his

eyebrows. Whenever he tried it he ended up with two bushy shrubs on his face.

Wizz was helping Tibben train. She was a Gatherer – a very rare and special gift – and she could find all kinds of hidden ingredients that no other creature could find.

Today Tibben was practising making Dig Fast Mix. It was the most popular potion at this time of year, when all the creatures liked to hide their food for the winter and dig their shelters. Wisgar, the Specs Mole, had already made a special trip above ground to ask for it, and a little Star Mouse had come in squeaking for a teeny tiny vial of the potion.

"Right, Tibben," said Grandpa, "I've made two lots of Dig Fast Mix. Now it's your turn."

Tibben reached under the counter and pulled out a heavy red book with golden writing. This was The Book of Potions, and inside were pages and pages of recipes and lists of ingredients. Tibben flicked through until he found it:

Dig Fast Mix

EFFECT:
Increases digging speed by 1000 times for one hour

INGREDIENTS:
Quick Sand, Strong Thorn

"Hmm . . . Quick Sand . . ." he said. "I know that's here somewhere . . ." His eyes scanned the shelves of the Potions Shop.

Wizz jumped up. "Wizz get!" she cried, and in a flash she had lifted down a bright green jar with her tail.

"Sand wooz," she said proudly. She had gathered the Quick Sand herself at Mouse Pond, when they went to help the River Horse.

"Thanks, Wizz." Tibben carefully sprinkled it into his Mage Nut training bowl. "Um . . . where's the Strong Thorn? I can never remember."

Wizz leaped up and came back

with a purple spiky plant in her
paws.

"You're so fast!" Tibben shook
his head in amazement. He peeled
off the purple bark, watching out
for the spikes, and mushed it into
his bowl.

Wizz peered over his shoulder.
"Purple-purple weez?" she said.

"Er, yes, it is a bit purple." Tibben
looked over at Grandpa, who was
whistling and pretending not to
notice. "Oh well, here goes . . ."
He tipped the crunchy mixture
into his mouth and swallowed as
fast as he could.

In an instant his hands started
to move.

"Yes!" he cried. "It's working!"

"Woozoo!" cried Wizz.

But Tibben's hands didn't look like they were digging. They were just jumping back and forth in tiny little movements.

"Huh?" he said.

Grandpa smiled and gave him a ball of wool. In no time at all Tibben had made a lovely warm jumper for Wizz.

"What's going on?"

Grandpa ruffled Tibben's hair. "You've made a wonderful *Speed Knit Powder* there," he said. "Can you make me a new hat?"

Tibben scowled but his hands carried on.

By the end of the hour he had made three new jumpers, six hats and a tea cosy.

He sat down, exhausted. Grandpa and Wizz were still laughing and dancing around in their new hats. Tibben smiled at them. He had to admit, the little purple bobbles on the top really were a work of art.

From the creators of the bestselling
Fairytale Hairdresser series,
Abie Longstaff and Lauren Beard

The
**Magic
Potions
Shop**

The
Young
Apprentice

Deep in the heart of Steadysong Forest
stands a very special tree; inside its trunk
you'll find the **Magic Potions Shop**.

It stocks every kind of potion:
Shrinking Potion,
Exploding Powder
and even Flying Potion!

Tibben is learning to be a Potions Master,
like Grandpa. He tries hard to help all the elves,
sprites and goblins who come to the shop –
but things don't always go to plan . . .

And when he sets out to help creatures on the
other side of the kingdom, will he remember
everything he's learned?

Also by Abie Longstaff and Lauren Beard

The Fairytale Hairdresser

Kittie Lacey is the brave heroine who's
not afraid to stand up to wicked witches
and evil queens to help her friends!

Discover this full-colour world, packed
with your favourite fairytale characters –
can you spot them all?

The Fairytale Hairdresser and the SUGAR PLUM FAIRY

Abie Longstaff   Lauren Beard

The Fairytale Hairdresser and CINDERELLA

Abie Longstaff   Lauren Beard

Turn the page for lots of fun

Magic Potions Shop

activities!

Spot the Difference

There are five differences between the two pictures below – can you spot them all?

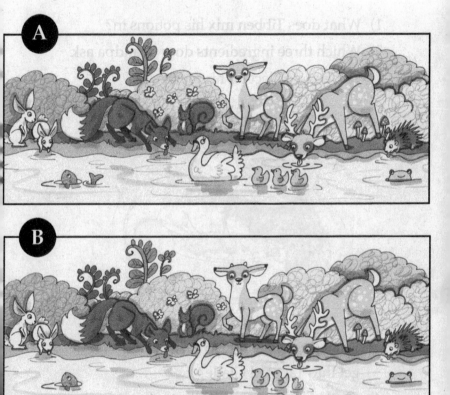

Turn to the back of the book for the solution to this puzzle!

Grandpa's Quiz

Test your knowledge – how many questions can you answer?

1) What does Tibben mix his potions in?

2) Which three ingredients does Grandpa ask Tibben to collect on his journey?

3) What do Tibben and Wizz pass through to get into Tangled Glade?

4) On their journey, which tasty snack does Wizz manage to find?

5) What had the River Horse lost from his hoof?

6) What had made the water in Lake Sapphire and Bubble River turn salty?

7) Which **Glint** does Tibben achieve after helping the River Horse?

8) What is Wizz's special skill?

Turn to the back of the book for the solution to this puzzle!

Word Search

The Kingdom of Arthwen is full of different kinds of creatures. There are ten hidden in this word search – can you find them all?

B	A	Q	P	Q	U	C	V	E	K	C	G	I	R	Q
C	H	B	B	I	E	K	N	T	B	A	I	P	X	J
U	N	Q	V	N	X	T	V	I	O	A	A	N	P	Z
Q	K	D	T	A	W	I	Y	R	L	V	N	H	H	X
M	F	A	I	R	Y	D	E	P	R	B	T	I	Z	R
E	U	F	L	E	Y	D	J	S	V	X	O	Q	X	L
R	I	N	O	Z	W	P	R	X	J	O	P	G	L	U
Y	J	R	M	R	F	G	M	K	U	M	K	O	D	N
Y	G	I	F	L	U	J	K	V	C	G	R	M	N	L
C	M	Q	H	R	B	X	I	C	D	T	V	K	S	E
P	K	T	T	D	J	O	R	Q	M	Q	B	O	M	J
C	J	V	D	I	A	M	R	E	M	P	A	A	X	I
Z	T	R	D	H	U	E	G	L	F	O	M	Y	K	G
U	Z	M	N	W	R	B	Z	Y	F	I	T	C	O	F
O	M	F	A	E	B	J	Z	E	N	D	Q	U	H	E

CENTAUR   IMP
ELF   MERMAID
FAIRY   PIXIE
GIANT   SPRITE
GOBLIN   TROLL

Turn to the back of the book for the solution to this puzzle!

Follow the Trail

Wizz is looking for *Secret Kelp* but there are so many interesting plants and creatures in the Tangled Glade that she keeps getting distracted! Can you help her follow the trail to find what she needs?

Turn to the back of the book for the solution to this puzzle!

Solutions

Spot the Difference

Grandpa's Quiz

1) His **Mage Nut** bowl
2) *Mothers Kiss*, **Red Clay** and *Mouse Water*
3) Through the Vine Curtain
4) **Honey Berries**
5) A *Moon Pearl*
6) The River Horse's tears
7) *Opal*
8) Gathering

Word Search

B	A	Q	P	Q	U	C	V	E	K	C	G	I	R	Q
C	H	B	B	I	E	K	N	T	B	A	I	P	X	J
U	N	Q	V	N	X	T	V	I	O	A	A	N	P	Z
Q	K	D	T	A	W	I	Y	R	L	V	N	H	H	X
M	F	A	I	R	Y	D	E	P	R	B	T	I	Z	R
E	U	F	L	E	Y	D	J	S	V	X	O	Q	X	L
R	I	N	O	Z	W	P	R	X	J	O	P	C	L	U
Y	J	R	M	R	F	G	M	K	U	M	K	O	D	N
Y	G	I	F	L	U	J	K	V	C	G	R	M	N	L
C	M	Q	H	R	B	X	I	C	D	T	V	K	S	E
P	K	T	T	D	J	O	R	Q	M	Q	B	O	M	J
C	J	V	D	I	A	M	R	E	M	P	A	A	X	I
Z	T	R	D	H	U	E	G	L	F	O	M	Y	K	G
U	Z	M	N	W	R	B	Z	Y	F	I	T	C	O	F
O	M	F	A	E	B	J	Z	E	N	D	Q	U	H	E

Follow the Trail